Pep Masalan
AND THE FLYING CARPET

Rosanne Hawke

ILLUSTRATED BY
Jasmine Berry

Pepper Masalah and the Flying Carpet

Text © Rosanne Hawke, 2023
Illustrations © Jasmine Berry, 2023

978-1-76111-110-5

Published by Wombat Books, 2023
PO Box 302,
Chinchilla QLD 4413
Australia
www.wombatrhiza.com.au

A catalogue record for this
book is available from the
National Library of Australia

Pepper Masalah

AND THE FLYING CARPET

For Markus

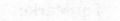

Pepper Masalah received her first name when Pepper's young human, Zamir Wali, saw her in the animal rescue shelter. She was as black as cracked pepper. 'Pa,' he cried, 'look at her copper eyes. She's a mini panther. Can I take her home, please?' He hugged Pa and made him smile.

'Why not, Zam,' Pa said.

Pa is Zam's father and he is sad most of the time. Pepper can smell it on him like a damp hessian bag. She thinks it must be because he doesn't have a mate. Zam is motherless, like Pepper, and they all live with Dadi, Zam's grandmother.

Dadi came from a country far away even before she had Pa. When Pepper first licked up the curry off Zam's plate, Dadi said, 'Hoi, Pepper is a spicy cat to suit a raja.'

Pa chuckled and stroked Pepper's sleek back. 'So you like masalah, Pepper?'

'Mirrep,' Pepper said.

That's how Pepper got her second name.

They live on a farm that has a thousand olive trees. One tree by the house is so huge it towers over the roof. It's exciting to climb. Pepper is a farm cat and she helps Zam round up the chickens. Every morning Pepper jumps on Zam's bed and waits until he yawns. Then she purrs in his ear asking for breakfast.

Zam always smiles. 'Purring is my favourite sound,' he says, 'and I can tell what you want, Pepper. You could talk if you had the right vocal cords.'

'Mirrep,' Pepper says. That's what it sounds like to Zam, but really Pepper said, 'Yes, I can talk and you'd hear if you had the right ears.' Actually, Pepper suspects that Zam has a way with animals and birds. It's like he almost understands her and when Zam whistles to parrots they listen and reply. He can sound like a crow, a kookaburra, and a young magpie. Even the chickens come promptly when he calls. It's fun being with Zam because he cares about creatures.

After the jobs are done, Pepper likes sleeping on the carpet in front of the fire or under the fan if it's hot. Funny thing about the carpet—it hums.

Zam says it has a thrumming sound as if the carpet has a heart. It makes Pepper feel warm and purry. But it makes Zam ask his grandmother about it before dinner time.

'Dadi, why does the carpet feel like it is alive?'

'Zamir,' she always uses his full name, 'this carpet is truly alive, but it is asleep. It has been in our family for many years. Just like your Dada's watch.' She lifts her chin at the watch Zam always wears. 'This carpet once belonged to a Kashmiri raja.' Dadi pauses to see if Zam is listening.

'This was when carpets could fly.' Dadi says that with a straight face but Pa winks at Zam. Dadi is full of interesting stories. None of them could be true, but she never smiles as if she is telling a joke like Pa does.

'There is a legend about this carpet,' Dadi adds. Both Pepper and Zam stare at the carpet. It looks ordinary, mostly red and blue—though it looks pale green to Pepper—with lots of patterns.

'This carpet, given the chance, will try to find its way back to Kashmir to its master. Only flying carpets can do this.' Pepper checks Dadi's eyes.

She seems serious.

'If you sit on it, you must shut the window or the wind will wake it.' She stares at Zam. 'Did you hear me, Zamir?' He nods. 'If the wind comes in you must jump off the carpet.'

Zam sits on the carpet with Pepper in his arms while Dadi makes curry in the kitchen. 'Dadi sure is a good storyteller, Pepper. She can make anything sound true.'

1
THE
STORM

In the autumn, a fierce storm blows up. Zam's father finishes cleaning the gutters and Pepper bunches up on the carpet in front of the fire. She doesn't like loud noises so Zam sits stroking her. Pepper doesn't even purr. Often, she purrs when she's scared to cheer herself up, but right now she is beyond scared. The wind howls so much the windows rattle and the trees toss their heads. There is an extra strong gust of wind and a branch from the giant olive tree breaks off with a huge crack. It smashes right through the lounge window. Glass shatters across the floor and the wind whooshes inside. Zam and Pepper are so shocked they forget what Dadi told them. They forget to jump off the carpet.

The wind flicks up the carpet with Zam and Pepper and whisks them out into the storm.

'Yeow!' Pepper doesn't like rain so she digs her claws into the carpet. She looks over the edge – it looks close enough to jump onto the tree. She readies herself to leap.

'Nooo!' Zam grabs her around the middle just as her paws leave the carpet. Zam pulls her back as she scrabbles to find a foothold. They are higher than she thought.

Zam tries to manoeuvre the carpet over the garden. 'Maybe it will lose height and glide onto the lawn. Then we can run back inside.' It doesn't work. The wind is so strong it lifts the carpet higher and higher, until the carpet rides the wind above the clouds. Zam and Pepper scream for help and howl—that's Pepper—but no one hears them.

Zam and Pepper peer down and Pepper jumps back in terror. She almost loses her grip on the carpet. She digs her claws in again and the carpet humps in the air.

'Whoa!' Zam holds on to Pepper. 'This is too high. If we fall from here, we'll die.'

Pepper howls again.

'That won't help,' Zam says. 'In this wind,

no one can hear us. Brrr.' He rubs his hands together as the wind whistles past his head. 'Chilly, isn't it?'

After a while, Pepper sits carefully, her ears flat against her head. Zam kneels beside her. 'At least it's flying straight and not up and down. I think that would make me sick.'

'Miaw.' Pepper checks Zam's face. He looks more relaxed. Maybe they won't die after all.

'What will Pa and Dadi think? That we got lost in the storm? No one saw us get taken by the wind.'

'Mirrp.' Pepper doesn't feel like thinking about it. She likes the farm and being on solid ground, not in the sky which is just for birds.

'I can't believe it,' Zam says, 'we're flying. Like an eagle.'

They zoom away from the storm, far away from the farm and paddocks and scrub, over the next town, over the red desert, until they see the ocean. That's what Zam calls it. To Pepper it looks like a never-ending dam.

The carpet flies faster and doesn't stop. The thrill of flying soon wears off and they sit, stiff with apprehension. Pepper prefers small places where she can curl up in, like the basket Pa uses for old newspapers. And here they are, still high in the wide, open sky. Pepper risks another peek over the edge. She can't even see the ground. She lets out a moan.

Zam checks around to see if he can stop the carpet. None of the patterns do anything when he presses them. 'I don't want us to land in the sea,' he says. Pepper narrows her eyes at him. 'I know you don't care for

so much water, Pepper.' Zam gives her a pat.
'And without a life jacket neither do I.'

Pepper's tail curls around her ears and
she fluffs out her fur to keep warm. At least
she has Zam. He was the one who saved her
when she was a kitten and even though she

feels older than him now, he is still all she needs to feel safe. Zam lies beside her and she rubs her head against his cheek. 'Mirrap,' she says with her eyes shut.

'Pepper, that sounded a lot like "take a nap".' Pepper opens one eye, that's what she did say. How odd.

'Maybe when we wake we will be back home,' Zam said. 'This has to be a dream.'

2
LANDING

They wake with a jolt. 'Oh no! It isn't a dream.' They are still flying, but the carpet is acting strangely. It slows and lurches every few metres. Pepper jabs her front claws into the carpet to keep from slipping off. Zam clutches onto the sides. When they look down, the sun is peeking over the horizon, and the ocean is gone. But there is a sea of yellow dunes that stretch as far as they can see.

The carpet flies lower. The ground is rushing by so fast Pepper hides her eyes with her tail to stop vomiting. Then the carpet tries to land. It hits the sand once and lifts into the air again.

'Whoa!' Zam holds on tight. 'Bet this is what a plane crash-landing feels like.'

The carpet tries again. It bunches itself up like a worm and glides down. What a bump! Pepper hangs on with her back claws as well.

This time the carpet lies flat on the ground. Pepper withdraws her claws and Zam stands up carefully. The carpet doesn't move. Zam wobbles across it to the sand.

'It's difficult to walk straight after riding a flying carpet all night.' He stares at the dunes towering above. 'What do we do now?'

Pepper giggles. 'Mirreg, you have carpet legs.'

Zam looks all around him. 'Who said that?'

'You heard me? I can't believe it.' Pepper's tail shoots straight up.

'There's nowhere for anyone to hide.'

Zam even checks under the carpet. 'Pepper, who's talking?'

'Mirray, it was me.'

Zam stares at her. 'Pepper? You can talk? I didn't expect you to answer me.'

Pepper sighs. She often miaowed to Zam at home but she didn't believe he would understand her one day.

'I was just talking as usual and you understood me this time,' she says.

Zam scratches his head. 'I think this carpet has pickled our brains.'

'Uh-oh.' Pepper springs to her feet.

'What's wrong?'

'I can feel thumping.' Pepper's fur rises as she watches the ground. The air is hot even though it is early. Zam takes off his jacket and Pepper stalks around the carpet, sniffing the air with her mouth open. Something big must be making that thumping sound and it's heading for them.

Zam keeps both feet on the carpet in case it flies off again. 'I don't want us left in a strange place by ourselves.'

He doesn't see the boy running across the sand. 'Look out!' Pepper howls.

The boy doesn't notice them either for he trips on the carpet. Pepper manages to spring out of the way but the boy knocks Zam over.

'Shuhada. What is this?' The boy sprawls onto the carpet beside Zam. He groans and rubs his leg. The boy wears a long white shirt to his ankles and a small white cap and he is taller than Zam. He smells different too and Pepper steps backwards. She swishes the tip of her tail from side to side.

The boy opens his eyes and sees Pepper first. 'A sanoor, a cat! You tripped me.'

Everything grows stranger. Pepper should not be able to understand the boy for he is speaking a different language. Zam seems to understand him too.

'That isn't fair,' Pepper says. 'I didn't trip you. You tripped on my carpet.'

'Yes,' Zam agreed. But the boy doesn't even

look up, just checks the scratch on his knee.

'Come on,' the boy says to Zam as he stands. 'This is a good carpet. Fancy finding you and a carpet in the desert. This is my lucky day. It will bring a lot of money in the souk and help my family.' He hands Zam his jacket.

Pepper jumps up in alarm. 'Miaow. No! You can't take my carpet.'

But the boy takes no notice of Pepper. 'Stop yowling, cat.'

Zam tries too. 'You can't have the carpet. It's ours.' But the boy doesn't understand Zam either.

The boy rolls up the carpet. Then he tucks it under his arm. He strides off so quickly that Pepper and Zam have to run to keep up with him.

3
HAMOOD

The boy's house is over the next dune. It's not as big as Zam's farmhouse, and it's made of mud bricks. Palm trees sway and other houses nearby show signs of activity. 'It's like a little village,' Zam says. There are chickens scratching around in the sand but Pepper knows not to bother them. Lots of other boys in long white shirts are pulling buckets of water from a canal that runs between the palms. When they see the boy with the carpet under his arm, they come running.

'Omar, what have you found?' They see

Zam and laugh at his jeans. The boys start to follow Omar and Zam into Omar's house, but there isn't enough room.

One boy tries to pull Pepper's tail but she hisses at him and glares like a black leopard. The boy isn't frightened. Pepper wishes she could climb a tree out of reach but she has to help Zam keep an eye on the carpet.

Inside, Omar rolls out the carpet in front of his father sitting on a couch. The man has a cast on his leg. He sucks in his breath. 'I've never seen a carpet like it.' He leans over to study the knots on the back. 'Look how rich the red is and yet it is very old.'

Zam frowns at the man's interest. 'It came from Kashmir,' he says. 'It belongs in my family.'

In a flash Pepper squirms through the boys' legs in the doorway and pounces on the carpet. 'It's mine.' No one answers but a boy younger than Omar stares at her as if she's grown two tails.

Then Omar's mother hurries into the room and sees the younger boy. 'Go get the water from the canal, Hamood. Your brother forgot.'

'I brought a carpet instead,' Omar says. 'This pagan boy was there too.'

'We are from Australia and this is our carpet,' Zam says firmly.

The man just stares at Zam.

Pepper prowls around the carpet. 'They can't understand the way we talk,' she says.

Zam frowns at Pepper. 'Then how come we can understand them?'

Pepper's tail flicks. 'I have no idea.'

'Look at that cat,' the father says. 'I've never seen one so shiny and well fed. Such big eyes. Like setting moons.'

Pepper washes her face and ears, paws, and bottom. That feels better. 'Did I hear food mentioned?' she says hopefully.

'Aboui, my Dad, I could sell the carpet and buy us a goat,' Omar says. 'Then we will have milk to drink and to sell.'

His father strokes his beard. 'Hmmm. It should be worth a goat. He glances at Zam. 'I wonder how the boy and the carpet came to be in the desert. He is too young to own it.'

'I own it, it's mine,' Pepper howls.

'It is a gift from Paradise, Aboui,' Omar says. 'Let me take it and I will bring a nursing goat for us.'

'Hmmm,' his father says.

'No!' Pepper springs off the carpet onto the father's shoulders. Her claws rake the man's long shirt to keep balance. 'It's my carpet.' Then Pepper growls. If she was a real panther she would roar.

'And throw this cat outside. Are we looking after feral animals now?'

Omar grabs Pepper and flings her into the courtyard. Fortunately, she lands on four paws. Zam rushes out to check she's okay. 'Pepper.' He gives her a cuddle, but Pepper is too annoyed to enjoy it.

Just then Hamood struggles into the courtyard with a bucket of water. He sees Pepper and crouches beside her. Pepper ignores him at first.

'Sanoor, you can talk,' Hamood says. 'How can this be? Are you a jinn?'

Pepper has never heard of a jinn. She yawns. 'I don't know why you can hear me.'

'What if the carpet is making us hear you, Pepper,' Zam says, 'and allowing us to understand a different language?'

Pepper fixes a searching stare on Hamood. Can they trust the boy? Pepper hears the father telling Omar how much money to ask for the carpet.

'The carpet is mine,' Pepper quickly says to Hamood.

Zam shifts his feet uneasily. 'Actually, the carpet is Dadi's.'

Pepper chooses to ignore that. 'I've slept on it every day since I was a kitten. It flew from the farm on the wind and brought us here. Now we want to go home.'

'To Australia,' Zam adds.

'If Omar sells the carpet we will be stuck here,' Pepper says.

'How grown up you sound, Pepper,' Zam says.

'I'm not a kitten anymore, like you,' Pepper says. Zam's eyes grow wide.

Hamood considers Zam. 'Is the cat yours?'

'Yes,' Zam says. 'And the carpet belongs to us.'

Hamood gazes at Zam, obviously surprised he can understand Zam's words too. Then he says, 'There is magic around you.' He stands and takes the bucket of water inside. Pepper watches through the window, padding back and forth on the ledge. Her tail curls around the latch.

'Aboui,' Hamood says to his father, 'you cannot sell the carpet—it belongs to the boy

and the sanoor. God will help us some other way.'

'Sanoor? How can a cat own anything? And a boy?'

'Please think about it, Aboui. How did the carpet get in the desert? It must have dropped out of the sky.'

Omar laughs. 'Off the back of a camel more likely.'

Hamood isn't helping, so Zam whispers to Pepper, 'We have to do something, quick.'

Pepper springs up onto the flat roof. There is a square-shaped box that looks like a chimney. She peers down it. Her whiskers don't touch the sides, so she jumps in.

What a clatter. The father glances up. 'Hamood, get that cat out of the wind tower.'

'It just wants to be with the carpet, Aboui.'

Pepper leaps down on to the carpet. She flattens her ears and stares at everyone in turn and hisses. Let them try and get her off her carpet. Outside, Zam claps his hands.

Omar's mother brings the man a tiny cup of coffee. 'I don't like selling the carpet, but you can't work at the moment. We have no choice.'

The boys' father sighs. 'Very well. Take it to the souk, Omar.'

Omar kicks Pepper off the carpet to roll it. Her hackles rise, but Hamood lifts her and holds her close. Pepper purrs a moment and rubs Hamood's cheek with her head, then springs out of his arms to follow Omar.

'Mirraw, come quickly,' Pepper calls to Zam. 'We can't let the carpet out of our sight.'

4

IN THE
SOUK

The souk is so noisy and dusty that Pepper wishes she had a box to hide in. A camel roars nearby and she jumps straight into Zam's arms.

'It's okay, Pepper. You haven't met a camel before. They're a bit like big goats.'

Pepper spots goats in a pen being sold. She's seen different coloured ones on the farm. Chickens flap and squawk as Zam walks past. Men in long white shirts at stalls and small shops cook chicken kebabs and rice. Another man is cooking flat bread in ashes. He shouts, 'Buy true Bedu arbood.'

'Yum,' Zam says.

Pepper notices a huge bowl of yoghurt. Mmm. Dadi makes yoghurt. But they can't stop. Pepper jumps down and they follow Omar past a man hammering a copper pot over a fire. There are many stalls of silver jewellery. One man holds up a dagger. 'Khanjars, sharpened here,' he shouts. Pepper bounds after Omar and catches up to him at a fruit stall.

'How much are the dates?' Omar asks a man.

'For you, two dirhams a bag.' The man gives a date to Omar to try. Pepper miaows. She's hungry too.

'Mmm, I'll be back after I sell my carpet,' Omar says.

'My carpet,' Pepper points out but no one except Zam takes any notice.

Omar approaches a camel driver. He has a white cloth wrapped round his head. Zam

29

follows more slowly. 'Be careful,' Zam says to Pepper. 'The man may not be nice like Pa.'

'I have a carpet to sell.' Omar unrolls it at the man's feet. Pepper bounds on to it.

'So?' The man looks as though he doesn't care, but Pepper isn't fooled. That's the way she watches for mice outside the kitchen cupboard.

'The carpet is very fine,' Omar says.

'It's mine,' Pepper adds, but it does no good. Her words sound like miaowing to Omar and the man.

'It's worth a goat.' Omar's voice isn't so strong now. 'What about that goat behind you. We could swap.'

The man takes some coins from his pocket. 'This is what the carpet is worth.'

The coins don't cover Omar's palm. 'That can't be true. This is not enough for a goat,' Omar cries.

Zam sucks in a breath and whispers to Pepper. 'Maybe Omar will give us back the carpet now.'

'What can you do about it?' the man says to Omar. 'You have more money than you had this morning, be thankful.' The man looms closer, his voice quieter. Pepper flattens her ears and hisses. 'I am sure you didn't make this carpet, boy. I could call you a thief.' He looks at Zam then as if he is a thief too.

Zam shakes his head. There is no point in trying to explain it is his carpet. No one understands him except Hamood and Pepper.

Omar backs away. 'What about the cat? Have you seen such a sleek one?'

The man glances at Pepper. 'This cat? She'll make a good meal boiled up for the goat. Now off with you.'

'No!' Zam shouts. 'Pepper come to me. Quick.'

Pepper crouches on the carpet wondering if she heard correctly. Zam boils up mince for her and adds some masalah too. Did the man say, 'Boil the cat?'

'Pepper! Quick!' Zam rushes towards her.

Too late, Pepper springs to her feet but the man is quicker. He grabs her by the scruff.

'You are a heavy one. Never seen a desert cat like you before,' and he shoves her into a cage.

'Hey!' Zam leaps at the man. 'That's my cat.' The man pushes him aside. He slings Pepper's cage onto a camel and wedges it between two boxes. The carpet is thrown over the camel's back as well. Even the goat is tied on.

'You can't do this.' Zam pulls at the man's shirt. 'I am Zamir Kiran Wali, from Australia and we have to go home to my dad, he's lonely.'

The man grabs him. 'I don't know where you've sprung from, foreign boy, but you can work for me. In return I will feed you.'

Zam kicks out but misses the man's leg. 'You can't take me!'

The man drags him away. Zam twists to see Pepper hunched up in the cage. 'Don't worry, Pepper. I'll get you out.'

Pepper doesn't like Zam's chances. She also doesn't like the cage. At home she has a box with a door like this one but it has a sheepskin rug in it. Zam puts her in it to ride in the car to see his little cousins who chase her. This cage doesn't even have a blanket and it is too small. She can't even stand up in it. Her ears lay flat on her head while she checks for a hole. But there is no way out.

Then she hears the goat: she's crying. 'What's wrong with you?' Pepper is too grumpy and scared to be nice.

The goat doesn't seem surprised that a cat spoke to her. 'When the men get hungry, they will eat me.'

'The man said he will boil me up for you.'

'In all that fur?' The goat stops crying and peers at Pepper. 'Yuk! I don't mean to be rude, but I doubt you will taste good.'

'Where I come from goats eat grass and hay,' Pepper says, her ears sitting up in hope.

'I never see much grass,' the goat says, 'and often I have to eat what I can find. Old sandals even. You'd taste better than that, I expect.'

Pepper doesn't like the conversation so she changes it. 'We should escape. If you come back to Omar's house with Zam and me, his people will look after you. They need a goat for milk.'

'How can we escape? Look at you—in a cage, and I'm tied with rope. So is your boy.' Then she says, 'This camel driver is a bad man. Zam is his slave now. He will never escape.'

Pepper watches the man tie Zam onto a camel nearby. She likes a challenge and is not going to let some rope and a cage stop her from planning.

Zam stares back at her miserably. Pepper must hate that little cage. It looks like a birdcage. She had the same look in her eyes when he found her in the rescue shelter two years ago. Defiant but sad. What a clever and beautiful cat she is, what a loyal, dear friend. He tries to move his arms but they are tied too tightly behind his back, there is no way he can get a finger loose. A magic trick of escaping from rope that Pa showed him once was for hands tied in front. The rest of him is strapped to the saddle of the camel as well. How on earth can he rescue Pepper?

5
IN THE
DESERT

There is a shout. The camel driver calls 'Hoosta' and his camel lurches to her feet with Zam on the back. Many other camels do the same. All the camels carry huge boxes and bags. Pepper's camel swings his head around to look at her.

'Good day,' Pepper says politely. She yawns. Up close she likes the camel's big eyes and long eyelashes. He grunts at Pepper gently. It is late afternoon, after the heat of the day, and the string of camels walk out of the souk and through the sand dunes.

'Where are we going?' Pepper asks the goat.

'To another oasis across the desert. The men will sell their goods.'

Pepper's eyes close. The camel's rhythm is making her sleepy.

In the middle of the night, Pepper wakes. Her camel is kneeling and happily chewing his cud. Pepper presses her paws on the door of the cage but nothing happens. The goat edges closer and butts it.

'Hey! Careful. You'll push me off.'

'I'm just trying to help.' The goat butts the cage door again.

Two things happen. First, the cage starts to slip. 'Nooo—' Pepper falls, cage and all, onto the ground. 'Ouch!' Then, the door flies open. She streaks out and springs back onto the camel's back. 'Thank you, goat. Now let's untie your rope.'

She bleats. 'Save yourself. You have a chance now.'

'Not without you. There's a nice boy called Hamood who will love you very much.'

'Truly? When that camel driver sold my kid, I thought I'd never be loved again.' The hopeful look in the goat's eyes makes Pepper more determined than ever.

'Can you chew this rope?' Pepper pulls at the rope with her teeth while the goat chews it.

Just then Pepper sees a movement from

the corner of her eye—a small shape slips into the camel's grain bag. She pounces into the bag and catches it: a mouse. She bounces back to the goat. 'Sorry to eat in front of you,' she says out of the corner of her mouth, 'but I haven't had a meal in ages.' The mouse is quickly finished, without Pepper even playing with it first. Then she helps the goat again.

The moon rises high by the time the goat is free.

'Shhh,' Pepper says as the goat slithers to the ground and lands on her head. 'Ooph!'

The camel stares at Pepper and the goat. In the moonlight Pepper sees him smile. 'Could you please pull down the carpet,' Pepper says to the goat, who grabs a corner between her teeth.

'Gently.'

When the goat tugs, it falls and lands on top of her. 'Oh, how will I get it off?' She pulls

39

at it with her teeth.

'Leave it,' Pepper says, 'that's how we can carry it. Now for Zam.'

Zam wakes when the cage falls on the sand. His first thought is Pepper. Is she all right? The cage is open and he can't see her. He tries to rise, forgetting he was tied up again after he ate. Last night when the camel driver produced the rope, Zam remembered Pa's trick and put his clenched hands out in front of him for the man to tie him up. The man nodded. 'Good boy.' Zam does what Pa said, *Put your knuckles in front of you and keep your elbows wide so there is some slack between your wrists.*

Now, Zam twists his wrists back and forth just as Pa showed him, gradually making the rope looser until Zam can grab a piece with his teeth and pull it over one hand. He twists his wrists some more until another strand is loose enough for him to pull it over his other hand with his teeth. Finally, he can pull both hands free. Then he undoes the rope around his ankles. He looks around – everyone seems to be asleep. Only a few camels groan and grunt. He creeps across to Pepper's camel. He sees the carpet fall on to the goat.

'What are you doing?' Zam whispers.

'We are escaping,' Pepper says. 'How did you get loose? We were coming to save you.'

Zam grins. 'And I you.'

'Right then,' Pepper says. 'It's time to go.'

Zam grabs a water bag from the camel's saddle before they creep quietly to the edge of the camp. The desert is silent and dark, waiting for them.

 # 6
THE
GOAT

'We have to run,' Pepper says. 'When they find us gone they'll look for us.'

'Why would they look for a goat, a cat and a slave?' the goat asks.

Zam looks quickly at the goat. 'Did I just understand the goat?'

'Mirrip, you did.'

'They might want the carpet,' Zam says. 'That camel driver looked greedy when he first saw it.'

Pepper finds the tracks of the camels in the sand heading back to the oasis and they follow them. When the sun rises and sits on the edge of the sand dunes, the goat stops. 'Oh, we need a rest.'

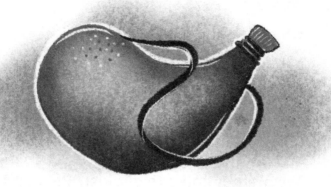

Pepper checks behind her. 'We can't stop for long.' The goat pants as Pepper inspects the carpet. Zam gives them both a drink from the bag. The water smells like hessian but Pepper manages to gulp it down without getting sick. She can't stand the smell of wet hessian bags. It reminds her of being a kitten again and of Pa and how sad and alone he smells.

'I'll carry the carpet,' Zam says. He rolls it up and balances it across his shoulders.

'Let's keep moving,' Pepper says.

They follow the camel string's tracks all morning, running when they can. In the afternoon a breeze springs up.

'Oh no,' the goat cries.

'What's wrong?' Zam asks.

'The wind will wipe the tracks away. We'll be lost out here. My great-uncle got lost in the desert. We never saw him again.'

'We are not going to get lost,' Pepper says firmly. 'Let's run as far as we can.'

The wind blows stronger and a corner of the carpet begins to flap on Zam's back.

The goat sees it and squeals. 'I think the carpet is alive.'

'That's silly,' Pepper says, then she feels sorry for the goat. 'It's just a carpet,' she adds in a softer tone. 'It flies on the wind.'

The wind is shrieking now, the sand shifts at their feet.

'The tracks,' the goat screams. 'I can't see the tracks.'

Pepper jumps onto the goat's back so they won't be separated. Zam holds onto her halter with one hand as they trudge through the sand against the wind.

Just then they all hear a sound. 'Sanoor! Sanoor!'

'It's a boy calling for a cat,' the goat says. 'We must be close to the oasis.' Then she adds. 'I might be imagining it.'

'I heard it too,' Zam says.

'How can we all imagine it?' Pepper asks.

Then she sees the boy through the driving sand. He has a long stick, and his nose is covered in a cloth. 'It's Hamood,' she cries 'Quickly, run to him, before we lose sight of him.'

Zam shouts, 'We're here.'

Hamood stands still. 'Is it you, sanoor? Zam?'

'Yes, and a goat for you to keep.'

When they reach Hamood he picks up Pepper and rubs his face against hers. 'Thank you for coming to help,' she says.

'When Omar said the caravan took you I thought I'd lost you forever,' Hamood says. 'But I came out a short way to call for you, hoping you had escaped.' Then he notices the goat. 'What a pretty goat.' She nudges his leg with her forehead.

Then another sound grows louder than the wind, a sound that thwacks through the ground. Pepper can feel it even in Hamood's arms. They all know what it is.

'One of the men has come on a camel to find us,' Zam says.

There is nowhere to hide. The camel will be onto them soon.

'Is it true you arrived on the carpet?' Hamood asks.

'Yes.' Pepper doesn't think it's a good time for conversation. She stares behind them. The thudding sounds much closer.

Hamood puts a hand on the carpet. 'Zam, lay the carpet on the sand. Get on, quickly.'

Pepper pounces on the square in the middle, the goat steps on carefully. Zam says, 'Will we all fit?' Hamood soon finds a spot and crosses his legs.

'It won't fly because we sit on it,' Pepper says. 'It only flies in a storm.' They all watch the carpet, but other than a corner curling up in the wind, nothing happens. Pepper wishes she could discover how it flies.

'Oh no, look!' Zam points.

A camel is galloping down a dune towards them. Pepper can see the rider. It is the camel driver who put her in the cage and kept Zam as a slave.

7
THE CARPET
FLIES AGAIN

'Fly, carpet!' Hamood shouts.

'It's no use,' Pepper says. 'There's no way to make it go or stop. It's just a carpet.'

Zam frowns. 'If it's just a carpet why did it fly in the storm?'

The camel driver can see them now, the camel is slowing. A sudden gust of wind blows across the sand. The carpet rises a few centimetres, then drops again.

'Aiwa, yes,' Hamood cries. 'You can do it. I know you can.'

A stronger gust makes Pepper's fur stand

on end. The goat falls onto her haunches. Pepper claws the carpet so she won't be blown off. Behind them, the camel sinks to her knees with a groan and the camel driver jumps down.

In desperation Pepper whispers, 'Please fly, carpet. We don't want to be eaten, or be slaves.'

Just then a whirlwind like a mini storm hurls the carpet into the air. The carpet hangs for a moment on top of the wind and sand, and then it flies, high enough to clear the camel driver's head and then it soars over the dunes.

'Aiwa, yes!' Hamood shouts. 'We're flying!'

'Wow!' Zam stares at Pepper, amazed. 'Did you just make the carpet fly?'

The goat cries but Hamood laughs. 'I've dreamt of this. I heard old stories about carpets that could fly, but I never thought to ride on one.'

Dadi told Zam and Pepper the same stories. And they hadn't even believed her.

Soon they see the date palms of the oasis. 'I hope the carpet can land,' Zam says.

Pepper remembers the crash landing in the desert when they arrived. The wind isn't as strong near the oasis and the carpet glides to the ground in the sand dunes just beyond the palms.

Hamood rolls up the carpet and they run through the souk, past mud houses and black goatshair tents until they stand puffing in the courtyard of Hamood's little house. Hamood ties the goat to the gate, then walks inside. Zam and Pepper enter as well, to keep an eye on the carpet. This time Pepper perches on Zam's shoulder to keep away from Omar.

'Aboui,' Hamood says to his father, 'I have found the boy, the cat and carpet. The cat and boy were bringing a goat for us.'

'A cat stole a goat?'

'They were treated badly. The cat rescued the goat.'

Hamood's father stares at Pepper in disbelief.

'Did I hear you have a goat?' Hamood's mother rushes into the room, then out to the courtyard. 'Oh! She is beautiful.' She brings the goat inside. 'What a good son you are.'

'It was the cat, Ummi, my Mum,' Hamood says. 'And the boy.'

'Whatever you say.' His father smiles at his wife stroking the goat.

Pepper thinks it is a good time to ask a favour. 'Could I sleep on the roof with the carpet, please?'

Hamood's father doesn't understand so Zam says to Hamood, 'Can you ask your father please?'

'Aiwa. Aboui, please may the cat and the

boy sleep with the carpet on the roof?'

'Very well, Hamood. But you can explain all this to your brother.'

Hamood carries the carpet up the stairs to the flat mud roof and lays it down. Then he picks up Pepper. She purrs and bumps her head against his forehead.

'I wish I could keep you forever,' Hamood says. He glances at Zam. 'You are very fortunate to have such a magical cat.'

Zam's eyes pop. 'Magical?'

'You won't stay, will you?' Hamood asks.

Pepper rests her head on Hamood's shoulder. 'We can't stay, Hamood, but I will never forget you.'

Hamood hugs Pepper one last time before setting her on the carpet. The wind is picking up again.

'We get very strong winds here,' Hamood says. 'They blow across the Sahara.'

'Please don't eat the goat,' Pepper says. 'She saved me.'

Hamood smiles. 'Laa, we'll drink her milk and let her have a kid.'

'She'll like that.'

Just then a sudden burst of wind blows the carpet off the roof. Zam hangs on and Pepper howls as the carpet drops. Hamood runs to the edge. 'Are you all right?'

'Yes,' Zam says. Before the carpet hits the ground, another gust of wind whips under it, bringing it level with the roof. It hovers in front of Hamood and he says to Pepper, 'Maybe that carpet does know what it is doing, sanoor. Listen to it, find its heart.'

The carpet is rippling as if it can't wait to go. 'Thank you,' Pepper says, 'but we must leave now.'

'Ma Salama, may you go with peace.' Hamood lays a hand over his heart.

'Goodbye,' Zam calls.

The carpet soars into the sky, turns in a circle once and then again.

'Doesn't it know where to go? Isn't Australia south of here?' Zam says. 'Oh, I feel queasy.'

Pepper whispers, 'Fly straight, please.'

The carpet streaks towards the evening sun.

Pepper Masalah's Cat Fact Files

- Pepper sleeps on and off for about 16 hours a day.

- When Pepper purrs it is due to air vibrating. It is felt as vibrations all over Pepper's body.

- Bombay cats like Pepper purr so loudly they can be heard in the next room.

- Loud noises are not only scary for Pepper but could hurt her sensitive ears.

- Pepper rubs her head on people and things when she wants to show other cats that they belong to her.

- Pepper swishes the tip of her tail from side to side when she is annoyed.

- Pepper's fur stands up (this is called piloerection) when she is scared. She also can hiss and spit if scared. These are signs of aggression so another cat doesn't guess she is scared.

- Pepper hates her tail to be pulled as it hurts. Since it is an extension of her spine, pulling it can dislocate it or cause paralysis of her back and hind legs.

Pepper Masalah's Cat Fact Files

- Pepper ignores other cats or people to be polite.

- Yawning is one of the ways Pepper uses to be friendly.

- Pepper's sense of balance and supple body give her the ability to land on her feet if she falls awkwardly.

- Pepper's whiskers act as feelers. They brush up against objects so Pepper can tell if she can fit into a space. If her whiskers don't touch the sides, she knows she can fit through. Because of this she hardly ever gets stuck in a hole.

- Pepper flattens her ears when she is angry.

- It is instinctive for Pepper to play with her live food before she eats it. This is from a hunting instinct to ensure that the food is fresh.

- Pepper has an accurate sense of direction and she can navigate by the sun.

- Pepper can see well in dim light.

BOY and CAT Disappear
IN FREAK STORM!

Olive grower, Mr Kiran Wali spoke to Herald correspondent, Alison Brown. 'Zamir is a happy boy who would never run away. And it is strange that his cat Pepper Masalah is also missing. She wouldn't have been out in the storm.

'Zamir and Pepper are adventurous, but for the carpet to be gone as well, they must have been stolen by someone. I don't understand it. Pepper is microchipped so it is odd no animal shelters have found her yet.'

STORM DAMAGE

When asked about the carpet Mr Wali said, 'The carpet is an antique that my parents brought with them from Kashmir years ago. My mother says it had once belonged to a king and it would always try to find its way home. Just a family legend of course.' Anyone seeing a dark-haired nine-year-old boy, with hazel eyes, a black Bombay/British shorthair cat, and a carpet are asked to notify the police immediately.

Read more in our next issue...

ZAMIR AND PEPPER

Comments

My cat disappeared when we were leaving to drive home from our holiday, 60 kilometres away. He arrived at our house 14 months later. He was okay except his feet were very sore. Please don't lose hope for your son. I will pray they return safely. Mariam.

Very sorry about your lost son. I have had many interesting experiences with cats, and I can assure you that your son's cat will bring him home. Nigel.

I'm so sorry to hear of the disappearance of your son and his cat. I have heard so many stories of cats coming home if they are lost, sometimes years later. I hope your boy can find his way home too. Suzi.

WORD LIST

Words are Arabic from the Arabian Peninsula unless otherwise stated.

Aboui	my Dad (pronounced a-boo-ee)
aiwa (aywa)	yes
arbood	a type of Bedouin flat bread cooked in ashes
Dada	Grandfather, father's father (Urdu) pronounced Daa-da
Dadi	Grandmother, father's mother (Urdu) pronounced Daa-dee
dirham	a coin worth about 35

	Australian cents.
hoi!	an exclamation
hoosta!	a command to tell a camel to sit or to stand.
khanjar	dagger
laa	no
masalah	spice—some curries are called masalah, e.g. chicken masalah. (Urdu/Hindi)
Ma Salama	goodbye, may you go in peace.
Ummi	my Mum (pronounced om-ee)
raja	king (Urdu/Hindi)
shuhada	What is this? (pronounced shoo harda)
souk	market
sanoor	cat

THANK YOU

A huge thank you to Brooks Glett for your excellent help with local Arabic in UAE & Oman. Thank you, Emma Reich for helping me find Pepper Masalah's name.

Thank you, Lachie McDonald for all your tips and ideas, also, Zac Zajac, Jane Jolly's class, St Mary's in Glenelg and many other students during Bookweek who loved Pepper Masalah's story.

Read *Pepper Masalah and the Temple of Cats* to discover where the carpet lands next.

ABOUT THE AUTHOR

 ROSANNE HAWKE has authored over 30 books for children and YA. She has been a teacher, an aidworker in Pakistan & the UAE, and a lecturer in Creative Writing.

Her books explore cultural and social issues, history, mystery, family and faith. She often writes of displacement, belonging and reconciliation and tells stories of children unheard. Many of her books have been longlisted, shortlisted or won awards in Australia and Cornwall. Her novels include *Shahana: Through My Eyes* and *Taj and the Great Camel Trek*, winner of the 2012 Adelaide Festival Award for Children's Literature, shortlisted in the Patricia Wrightson Prize and Highly Commended in the Prime Minister's Literary Awards.

She is the 2015 recipient of the Nance Donkin award and is a Carclew, Asialink, Varuna, and May Gibbs Fellow. Rosanne is a Bard of Cornwall and lives in country South Australia in an ancient Cornish farmhouse with underground rooms.

Pepper Masalah
and the
Temple of Cats

The carpet lands in the River Nile. After Pepper has a run-in with a crocodile, she and Zam are taken to a temple to be safe. Here cats are revered and Pepper most of all. She is so special the attendants want to make a mummy of her.

www.wombatrhiza.com.au